June Mountain Secret

June Mountain Secret

Nina Kidd

HarperCollins*Publishers*

Thanks to Linda Zuckerman for faith, hope and help. And thanks
to George Stroud of The Nature Conservancy for information about
the McCloud River Preserve, the setting of this book. The McCloud's
2,330 acres in Northern California are part of the many wild lands
and waters the Conservancy protects worldwide, in trust for us all
to study and enjoy as long as we leave them as we find them.

JUNE MOUNTAIN SECRET
Copyright © 1991 by Nina Kidd
Printed in the U.S.A. All rights reserved.

Library of Congress Cataloging-in-Publication Data
Kidd, Nina.
June mountain secret / Nina Kidd.
p. cm.
Summary: Jen and her father go up a mountain stream and spend the
day fishing for wild rainbow trout.
ISBN 0-06-023167-X — ISBN 0-06-023168-8 (lib. bdg.)
[1. Fishing—Fiction. 2. Fathers and daughters—Fiction.]
I. Title.
PZ7.K5313Ju 1991 90-31574
[E]—dc20 CIP
AC

Typography by David Saylor
10 9 8 7 6 5 4 3 2 1
First Edition

Mayfly nymph

For David and Daryll

It was spring.

In the dark of the morning Jen and Dad packed their reels, rods and flybox. They put on wide hats for shade and high boots for wading.

Then, before dawn, they were gone—hunting rainbows up a June mountain.

As the sun rose, they climbed far upstream and looked
for a pool that might hide one. But this run was too
shallow; that one dropped too fast; and this one, they
agreed, was too bright.

At last, there it was: a pool with a secret, a translucent pool slipping sleek in the shadows. Jen held her breath. All she heard was faint rushing on creekstones. All she saw was the gleam on a ripple. Then . . .

Cloop!

"A trout!" whispered Dad. "Hunting mayflies."

"There!" Jen jumped up. "There he was, by that rock!"

More mayflies sailed down, but the water was quiet.

"Oh, he must have seen me," said Jen, "and now he's down, hiding."

"Well, let's wait a bit," replied Dad, "and catch one of those mayflies." If a trout hid from Jen but swam up to eat mayflies, then, he said, they would try to fool him.

White Alder

California Sister

Mayfly duns

Yellow-Bellied
Sapsucker

Western Azalea

Sedge

Western Toad

Horsetail

Indian Rhubarb

Jen found a live mayfly, caught in a spiderweb.

She brought the mayfly back. Inside Dad's flybox were
two that just matched it: the same size and same color, only
Dad's were made of feathers and thread, on a hook.

"Let's rig up," Jen said.

Jen fished . . . and she fished.

Fly rod

Fly line

Safari hat

Polarized sunglasses

Fly reel

Fishing vest

Rubberized
hip waders

Cleats

Slippery rocks

At last she splashed up the bank. "There! I quit. I don't even want him!" She made a face at the pool, but the trout just laughed.

Cloop!

"Well," said Dad, "let's have lunch."

*Golden Stonefly nymph**

*Mayfly nymph**

They stretched out in the sun, and the sandwiches,
apples and strawberry pies did taste good.

The stream moved by slowly, fish resting below, so quiet
that all seemed to sleep on the mountain.

*Hellgrammite (Dobsonfly larva)**

*Caddis larva (in its case)**

Except Jen. She climbed up a tree, and slid down a
boulder, and found a big salamander. And she almost forgot
she was mad at the trout stream.

*Approximately twice life size

When Dad woke up, there were dark flies on the water.
"Time to think like a trout! Want to try?" he asked Jen.
"No!" she said.
But she brought him the flybox and picked out a dark-
speckled mosquito.

So Dad cast. The fly came down gently, and while she
watched it, Jen felt Dad slip the rod and line into her hands.
The fly rode by a rock, and Jen felt Dad step back. There
must be a trout watching . . . right . . . about . . . there.

Cloop!

It was a wild rainbow.

Holding him now, Jen was part of the secret, the secret of rainbows that hide in the river.

To keep the secret alive, he must be free. They unhooked him gently; he slipped down, slipped away and was gone, back to his home, cool and safe in the river.

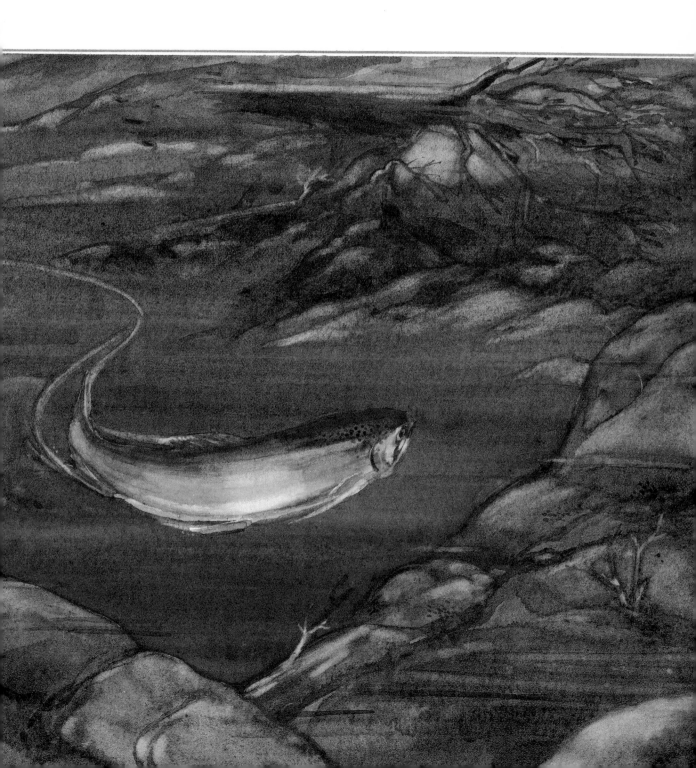

As they walked down the trail in the evening, Jen heard streams in the dark, and Dad saying, "Good work!"

And she thought of the mayflies and strawberry pies and the secret she shared with a rainbow, a wild trout that hides up a June mountain.

Note

Many wild trout streams today are threatened by dams and pollution. And every year, more people are fishing. In some places, to be sure there will be enough fish for the coming season, people must limit the number of fish they catch. In other places, there are so few fish left that people must raise new trout in tanks and release them in streams.

Fly fishing, an idea thousands of years old, is especially important now because artificial flies, like the ones Jen and Dad used, allow the fisherman to release the fish unharmed. A trout will not swallow an artificial fly. The fish realizes it is not good to eat, and the hook only fastens itself to the edge of his hard jaw. The careful fisherman can land him unharmed, and then either keep the fish or set him free again.

The McCloud River in California, where Jen and Dad fished in this book, is real. McCloud rainbow trout have lived there for thousands of years. On the stretch of river owned by The Nature Conservancy, all fishing must be done with flies or lures, and all fish caught must be set free. In that stream the wild rainbow trout will remain, and their offspring will be there for our children to enjoy in years to come.